PRAIRIE SCHOOL

story *by* **AVI**

pictures *by* **BILL FARNSWORTH**

HarperCollinsPublishers

In memory of Jane Wright

—A.

For my best friend, Deb

—B.F.

HarperCollins®, 📖®, and I Can Read Book® are registered trademarks of
HarperCollins Publishers Inc.

Prairie School
Text copyright © 2001 by Avi
Illustrations copyright © 2001 by Bill Farnsworth
Printed in the U.S.A. All rights reserved.
www.harperchildrens.com

Library of Congress Cataloging-in-Publication Data
Avi
    Prairie school / by Avi ; pictures by Bill Farnsworth
      p.   cm.
    "An I can read chapter book."
    Summary: In 1880, Noah's aunt teaches the reluctant nine-year-old how to read as
they explore the Colorado prairie together, Noah pushing Aunt Dora in her wheelchair.
    ISBN 0-06-027664-9 — ISBN 0-06-027665-7 (lib. bdg.)
    [1. Books and reading—Fiction.   2. Aunts—Fiction.   3. Prairies—Fiction.
4. Wheelchairs—Fiction.   5. Physically handicapped—Fiction.   6. Colorado—Fiction.]
I. Farnsworth, Bill, ill.   II. Title.
PZ7.A953 Pr   2001   00-38834
[Fic]—dc21

1 2 3 4 5 6 7 8 9 10
❖
First Edition

CONTENTS

Chapter One   The New Land   4

Chapter Two   Aunt Dora   9

Chapter Three   One Week   13

Chapter Four   Prairie School   21

Chapter Five   The Stars   27

Chapter Six   Learning   30

Chapter Seven   Some Good Luck   35

Chapter Eight   Last Lessons   43

Chapter One
The New Land

In 1880 the Bidsons moved from their worn-out farm in Maine to the new state of Colorado.

There, on the rolling prairie, they built a sod house, plowed the soil, planted seeds, and harvested wheat.

Noah, who was nine, helped with all the work. He hauled water and fed the animals. He made sure that the house was free of snakes and that the hearth fire stayed lit.

Now and again he got on the horse and wandered over the land. Free as a lark, he came to love the prairie.

One day Mrs. Bidson said to her son, "Noah, we're going to have a visitor."

"Who?" asked Noah.

"My sister. Your aunt Dora."

"I thought she teaches school back East."

"She's coming to give you schooling."

"Schooling!" Noah said. "Don't I work as hard as you and Pa?"

"Noah," said Mr. Bidson, "your ma and I can hardly read or write. We want you to do better."

Noah stormed out of the sod house. On the prairie he stared at the sky. "Reading is as much use on the prairie as the stars!" he cried.

Chapter Two

Aunt Dora

Two months later Noah and his mother drove their wagon to the nearest railway stop. It was twenty-five miles away. When the train halted, no one got off.

Noah grinned. "Guess Aunt Dora got smart and didn't come."

Then a wheelchair was lowered from the baggage car. Two men carried a lady from a passenger car and placed her in the chair.

"Dora!" Mrs. Bidson cried. "Is that you?"

"It's me, all right," Aunt Dora said.

"But what's happened to you?" her sister asked.

"Soon after you went West, a buggy I was driving turned over. I lost the use of my legs. I didn't write because I didn't want you to worry. I'm doing fine now, but your letter was a blessing. I needed a change."

Mrs. Bidson gave her sister a big hug.

"And this must be my student," Aunt Dora said to Noah. "Noah," she asked, "you ready for some learning?"

"Don't need no schooling on the prairie," Noah said.

"You're ready!" Aunt Dora said.

All the way home the two sisters talked about family. Noah said not one word.

Chapter Three

One Week

Monday

Aunt Dora set up her school in the sod house. A lamp was lit because it was so dim.

But then Noah went to fetch water from the creek two miles away. He took a long time coming back.

When he did, Aunt Dora pointed to the letter she had written on the board. "A," she said. "Please repeat that."

"A," Noah said. Then he stood up. "Aunt Dora, I forgot to feed the chickens."

Tuesday

When Noah came back from his morning chores, he sat in his chair and fidgeted.

At the blackboard Aunt Dora wrote the letter B. "This is B," she said. "Can you read it?"

Just then Noah saw a snake in the front yard. "Got to get that snake!" he cried. He didn't come back all day.

Wednesday

Aunt Dora wrote the alphabet on the board. She pointed to the letters with a stick. "Noah, can you find the letters for your name?"

"Nope."

"Noah, don't you ever want to read?"

"Nothing to read on the prairie," he said.

Thursday

Whenever Aunt Dora tried to teach, Noah

excused himself to do chores. He did them

as slowly as possible.

16

Friday

Aunt Dora put numbers on the board. "Would you like to learn to count?" she asked.

"Aunt Dora," Noah said, "it's too hot and dark to stay in here."

"Noah," Aunt Dora said, "you are as stubborn as a downhill mule on an uphill road."

Saturday

Aunt Dora was too upset to do any teaching.

Sunday

"I'm afraid my kind of schooling won't work here," Aunt Dora said to her sister and brother-in-law.

"Dora," her sister said kindly, "life out here is different."

"And I'm afraid," said Mr. Bidson, "our Noah has become a regular prairie dog."

Aunt Dora laughed. "Now I know what to do!"

Chapter Four

Prairie School

The next morning when Noah came back from hauling water, Aunt Dora had wheeled herself out of the sod house. On her lap was a book.

"Noah," Aunt Dora said, "push me around. I need to see this prairie of yours."

"The ground isn't flat," he warned. He wondered how her wheelchair would ride.

"Well, then, you'd best tie me in."

21

When Noah pushed Aunt Dora over the prairie, the chair jumped and rolled like a bucking horse. Aunt Dora held on.

"It's very beautiful here," she said. "What is the name of that yellow flower?"

Noah shrugged.

Aunt Dora looked through her book. "It's a dogtooth violet," she said, reading. "The only lily in this area. It grows from a bulb. The Indians boil the bulb and eat it for food."

Noah was surprised. "Is that true?" he asked.

Aunt Dora pointed to the page. "That's what it says here. Now show me some more prairie," she said.

All day Noah wheeled her around. All day Aunt Dora asked questions about what she saw. Noah told her what he knew. Each time, Aunt Dora looked in her book and told him more.

Noah was puzzled. "Aunt Dora, how come you're so smart?"

"I'm just smart enough to read," she said.

Chapter Five

The Stars

That night Aunt Dora asked Noah to take her outside. The night sky was full of stars.

"Noah," Aunt Dora said, "what do you see up there?"

"Stars," he said.

"I see stars too. But I can also see pictures."

"Pictures? Where?"

"There's the mighty warrior Hercules. There is a snake. There's the Big Dipper. Nearby is the Little Dipper."

Noah said, "Are you going to tell me you get all that from a book too?"

"Reading books only helps me under-
stand what I see and hear."

Noah hung his head. "There are no
books on the prairie."

"One of my trunks is full of books."

Noah said nothing.

"Noah," Aunt Dora said softly, "learn to
read and you'll read the prairie. What do
you say to that?"

After a moment Noah said, "I might
try."

Chapter Six

Learning

The next morning, beneath the bright sun, Noah sat at Aunt Dora's feet.

Aunt Dora handed him a book. "This is a primer," she said. "Your first reader."

Noah opened the book.

That week Aunt Dora had Noah practice learning and writing letters on a slate she had brought. There were times Noah worked so hard, his hand and head ached.

At the end of the week Aunt Dora said, "I have an announcement. Noah knows his letters."

Noah stood up nervously. Slowly, he recited the twenty-six letters. "Did I get them all?" he asked Aunt Dora.

"Every one."

Mr. Bidson was so excited, he smacked the table with his fist. Mrs. Bidson clapped her hands with joy.

Chapter Seven

Some Good Luck

Noah's life had changed. He still did some chores. His parents did the others so he could spend more time learning.

Some days Noah studied from the readers Aunt Dora had brought. Other days she asked him to wheel her out on the prairie. There she read him poems or stories. Sometimes she read facts about the land. More and more she asked him to read to her.

Two months later they were going over
a hill when Aunt Dora cried, "Stop!"

"What's the matter?" Noah asked.

Aunt Dora pointed. "There's a flower
we've not seen before. What is it?" She
gave Noah her flower book.

Noah looked at the flower, then he opened the book. "It is called a prairie bell," he read slowly. "It blossoms once a year. People who see it are said to have good luck."

Aunt Dora laughed. "Now, Noah, if you had never read that, you'd never know you were going to have good luck for the rest of your life!"

Four months later Aunt Dora asked Noah to read a poem called *A Psalm of Life* out loud.

When Noah finished, Mr. Bidson said, "That's the most powerful poem I ever heard." He had tears in his eyes.

Mrs. Bidson hugged Noah. Then she hugged her sister.

That night Noah lay in bed. He was too excited to sleep. He heard his mother say, "Our Noah is going to be a lot smarter than us."

"Makes you feel proud, doesn't it?" said his father.

From then on Noah always read to the family after dinner. Sometimes it was poetry, or a chapter from a story or history book. Sometimes it was from the Bible.

He read slowly at first. Often he needed help from Aunt Dora with words. Day by day he got better.

At times Noah was so happy with his reading, he would wander outside and gaze at the stars. It seemed as if they had all become pictures.

Chapter Eight

Last Lessons

One night Aunt Dora and Noah were outside looking at the stars.

"Aunt Dora," Noah said, "I found a new constellation."

"What is it?"

"It's called the Wheelchair. And you're sitting in it. See, it's those stars there." He named them.

"Noah Bidson!" Aunt Dora laughed. "When you see me up in Heaven, I guess it's time for me to get on home."

"Aunt Dora, I want you to stay and teach me more."

"But I need to get home before winter sets in," she said. "You've made a fine start, Noah. Now your best teacher will be yourself."

Noah grew thoughtful. "Aunt Dora, can I ask two questions?"

"Of course."

"Is it hard being in the wheelchair all the time?"

"It is."

"If you could get your legs to work by giving up all your books and reading, would you do it?"

Aunt Dora was quiet. Then she said, "Noah, my mind can go farther with books than my body can go with my legs. Having both—like you do—means you'll go twice as far."

Two weeks later Noah, his mother, and
Aunt Dora drove back to the railway stop.

Mrs. Bidson gave her sister a tearful
kiss.

When Noah gave Aunt Dora a hug, she
slipped him a letter. "Don't read it until
you get home," she whispered.

Noah got home late that night. He took
Aunt Dora's letter outside and read it
alone.

Dear Noah,

Right now I am on the train going East. You are beneath the prairie stars. But because you now can read and write, no matter how far apart we are, we can always talk to each other.

Your loving aunt,
Dora

That very night Noah sat down and wrote his first letter.

47

Dear Aunt Dora,
I live on the prairie, but I
can read the whole world.

Your loving nephew,

Noah